# ANGELA'S ALIENS

A Richard Jackson Book

INVESTIGATORS OF THE UNKNOWN
BOOK FOUR

# ANGELA'S ALIENS

## Janet Taylor Lisle

Orchard Books : New York

Orchard Books
95 Madison Avenue
New York, NY 10016

Manufactured in the United States of America
Book design by Mina Greenstein
The text of this book is set in 12 point New Aster.
10  9  8  7  6  5  4  3  2  1

Library of Congress Cataloging-in-Publication Data
Lisle, Janet Taylor.
Angela's aliens / Janet Taylor Lisle.
p.   cm.—(Investigators of the unknown ; bk. 4)
"A Richard Jackson book"—Half t.p.
Summary: Because Angela seems to have become
a totally different person and tells of being
abducted by aliens and living among them, her
friends become concerned about her.
ISBN 0-531-09541-X   ISBN 0-531-08891-X (lib. bdg.)
[1. Identity—Fiction. 2. Extraterrestrial beings—
Fiction. 3. Friendship—Fiction.]   I. Title.
II. Series: Lisle, Janet Taylor. Investigators of the
unknown ; bk. 4.
PZ7.L6912An   1996
[Fic]—dc20   96-12991

# ANGELA'S ALIENS

## chapter one

GEORGINA
Rusk was certain
what they had seen that night were helicopters.

She said they were helicopters at least ten times, until her friend Poco began to peer at her strangely.

"Are you sure?" Poco asked. "You can say if you're not."

"Trust me," Georgina said.

But of course Poco wouldn't.

There had been sightings near the old Wickham Reservoir before. It was one of those places where people saw things: spinning saucers and dancing points of light and shadows that hovered in the dark above the water. Over the years, all sorts of stories had grown up.

Poco said, "Remember those dogs they never found? The ones that disappeared from their own backyards? Mrs. Anthony from down our block thinks her Rambler was sucked up by a giant light beam."

"Oh, Rambler," Georgina said. "That yapping mutt. Someone let him out and strangled him probably. People will believe anything if you let them. And please don't bring up that stupid flying doll."

"Why not?" said Poco, who had just been about to.

In this strange tale, the doll of a younger girl they both vaguely knew had been surrounded by light before her eyes one night, and then floated out her bedroom window. The girl had insisted her story was true, though no one believed her—until two days later.

"They found the doll in a ditch," Poco recalled now, "far across town—too far to walk. It makes you wonder."

"About what?" Georgina asked.

"Well, what if aliens were after that girl but

somehow, in the rush, they picked up her doll. Then they saw their mistake and dropped it."

Georgina looked away, disgusted. "Sure, if you believe in aliens. Personally, I don't. They're not scientific. I think that little girl made everything up. She wanted attention and she got it."

"Scientific?" Poco squinted in her foggy way. "Does that mean what we saw was—"

"Nothing!" Georgina roared.

Poco Lambert had become an embarrassment that fall. The chief trouble was, she never seemed to grow and by now had turned into such a small person that Georgina disliked going about with her. Georgina was sure people would think she was younger than she was, or that, having no friends, she was settling for toddlers.

And there was something else: Poco's endless bird chats with a robin that lived in the Lamberts' backyard. Over the summer, Poco had grown more and more attached to him. She couldn't go for five minutes without wondering where he was or what he was doing, or if he was thinking fondly of her . . . which he never was, of course, being only a bird, with a brain fixed mainly on warm baths and worms.

"Poco, you can't expect him to feel anything

back!" (Georgina was forever having to cheer her friend up.)

"Really, Poco, don't worry, he'll come home again. He has not crashed into a sliding glass door!"

Eventually, he would return. Then he would parade in front of Poco's nose without a thought for the agonies she had suffered. But she was always so thankful to find him safe that she only tried harder than ever to please him, in hopes that he wouldn't go off again . . . which he did anyway. He was heartless. Heartless!

In fact, as Georgina might have pointed out, the bird was the reason they'd been awake that night, and had seen what they had in the still, black sky. Helicopters probably. Or was it something else?

## chapter two

POCO HAD
been sitting
rigid on her bed, keeping watch for the robin
out her window. Georgina, who was spending
the night, lay yawning beside her. Across town,
a church clock had rung twelve slow strokes,
each one answered by a dismal echo. Midnight,
times two. Poco stood up.

"He's always here by now. Something's happened, I know it."

"No it hasn't." Georgina yawned again. "I'm
sure he's all right."

"He's not. He's fallen. He's broken his wing."

"He'll be back by morning. Come on, let's go to sleep."

"George, how can you be so uncaring?" Poco whispered in a furious voice. Everyone else in the house had gone to bed hours ago. "I can't stand it anymore. I'm going out to find him."

"You can't do that! It's the middle of the night."

But Poco had done it. She had gotten up and tiptoed down to the kitchen, where she let herself out the back door. Georgina, as her guest, was forced to follow.

They stepped off the porch and walked across the grass, feeling strangely light in their summer pajamas. It was early September but still quite warm. Under the old apple tree, Poco came to a stop.

"George, hoist me up! I can't reach the branch."

"Okay, okay. Stop kicking."

"Sh-sh! Mom will hear. Just push me up . . . there! Now let me step on your shoulders. . . ."

"Okay, but wait. . . . Ouch!"

After this, there was silence, except for the noise of Poco scrabbling upward in the tree.

"Georgina, I can see his nest!"

"Good grief."

"He's not in it."

"Big surprise."

"I thought maybe he'd come home and fallen asleep at the bottom. Robins do that sometimes."

"Really." By now, Georgina had climbed up, too. She sat back indignantly on a branch. They were quite high off the ground, she noticed, glancing down.

"Let's just stay here for a while," Poco whispered from above. "Maybe, if he sees me, he'll figure out I'm worried and fly home."

"Oh sure."

"He does care about me, whatever you think."

Georgina did not even bother to argue. She turned her eyes upward to the stars and thought of going home. But her parents were away at an overnight party. That was why she was staying with Poco.

The air in the apple tree felt thick and still. The leaves made a latticework screen around them, through which the sky's vast depth was visible in patches. It was one of those nights when the eye opens wide and the mind slips its cage and makes for wilder regions. Georgina took a firmer hold on her branch.

Below, the yard shone dimly, illuminated by

a single light on the Lamberts' back porch. There was a shadow with a long-nosed profile on the lawn. Could it possibly be a wolf? A twig snapped in the underbrush.

"George, what's that?" Poco was pointing off to their right.

"What?"

"That creature. Slinking along the ground over there. It looks hairy."

Georgina turned and caught her breath. But then she let it out again. Poco's mind must have escaped into wild places, too; the hairy creature was only a cat. In fact, it was Poco's own, Juliette. The old Siamese appeared to be on a hunting expedition. She was moving slowly, head low to the ground. All at once, she leapt on a clump of bushes.

"Oh!" Poco gasped. Then she recognized her, too. "Oh, it's only Juliette."

"I think she's caught something." Georgina strained to see.

They heard the brutal sounds of a body being shaken and dragged farther into the underbrush. Most likely, it was one of the little chipmunks that lived along the yard's borders. Juliette had a taste for them.

Poco covered her face. "Don't think of it," she said.

The night fell into silence again. There was no moon. Except for the far-off prickle of stars, the sky beyond the leaves was blacker than a cave. Georgina shifted on her perch. A phantom claw of wind scraped through the tree, and in that instant, she felt something new. A premonition of movement rippled through the leaves, of clouds gathering or armies on the march. Georgina glanced up.

"Poco! Look!"

Above, a squadron of round, bright-lit objects hovered in silence, sharply etched against the night sky. Georgina and Poco leaned back and stared. Five . . . no, six . . . no, seven gleaming forms paused overhead in an investigative way.

"They're like glass marbles. You can see right through." Georgina's voice came out as a whisper.

"What's all that stuff floating inside? George, I think they can see us, too."

Georgina felt her eyes heat up. For a moment, it did seem as if the objects were staring down, had found them in the dark and paused to examine them. Then *zip*! Her spellbound eyes were released. The ghostly marbles flew away. Or melted. Or maybe vaporized? It was hard to find the word for what they had done. One second they were there, and the next, vanished.

"What were they?" Poco was cowering on the branch.

"I'm not sure."

"They looked like—"

"Don't say it." Georgina rubbed her eyes. "They were probably just planes. Or helicopters—that must be it."

"But they were so quiet."

"Sometimes spotlights catch on things in the sky and make them look completely different."

"It could have been a flock of geese migrating south. Or was it—" Poco stopped. "Oh no, robins! Maybe he's left for Florida."

"Come on," Georgina said, "let's start climbing down. I think I want to go in." She felt shaken.

"Will you help me watch again out my window?"

"Oh, Poco, he'll come back whether we watch or not. It's the one thing that bird does that's reliable."

"You're right." Poco sighed. "Why do I get so worried?"

"Because you're caught. You love him. You can't help it."

Georgina said this in such a faint voice that Poco looked down.

"George? Are you all right?"

There was no answer.

"George!"

"Yes, I'm okay. It's just so strange." Poco quickly climbed down beside her. Then they sat close together and stared up through the leaves, but the sky was vast and dark and unreadable.

## chapter three

THERE IS no place further from the trackless realms of night than an ordinary bedroom flooded with morning sun. Georgina woke up and glanced about with relief. Everything seemed back to normal. Poco sat hunched by the same window, but now her face was flushed with contentment.

"George, look, my robin's here." He was perched on a sprig of the apple tree, grooming his wings with self-important pecks. "He certainly believes in neatness."

Georgina sniffed. "He probably has lice."

From the foot of Poco's bed came a heave of cat fur. Old Juliette had come in with them last night and crept upstairs to her usual sleeping spot. Now she roused herself, padded over, and gazed with her powerful blue eyes out the window. Whatever she saw seemed to interest her, because a minute later she eased her big body off the bed and made for the door with a stiff-legged gait.

Juliette was not as quick as when she had first come to live with Poco. That was last fall, when Angela Harrall, Poco and Georgina's friend, had moved to Mexico with her father for a year. Unfortunately, Angela's parents had decided to get divorced, and then had gone off in very different directions.

Her mother was accepted at a famous law school in California. Her father bought into a South American business. There was no room in these plans for an aging cat, so Juliette was left behind with the Lambert family—where, shortly after, she was run down by a car in the street and then had disappeared for several mysterious weeks.

Juliette was quieter when she returned, and she had slept a great deal. Last summer, she'd collapsed twice from the heat, causing everyone to worry that her time was near.

"I hope Angela comes back soon, or she'll miss saying good-bye," Poco's mother was always murmuring sadly.

To which Poco would answer, "Not good-bye. Farewell. Juliette has a lot more lives to go on to." It was one of those notions she insisted on.

From under the covers, Georgina watched as the cat struggled by.

"Whatever life Juliette has coming up next, she's certainly turned into a wreck in this one. Angela will hardly recognize her," she said in a rather mean tone to Poco.

Juliette had always made Georgina nervous. The cat possessed a queer hypnotic stare that seemed at times to take control of people. And what was one to make of the tiny silver box that had appeared around her neck last winter? Georgina glimpsed it now as Juliette passed by. The box contained catnip, a strong-scented herb associated with ancient, vanished worlds.

"And she's so skinny," Georgina went on, sitting up more boldly as Juliette's tail disappeared into the hall. "Her shoulders stick out like two chicken wings. Angela will think she isn't being fed."

Angela this, Angela that. Lately, Georgina kept bringing her up. She had missed Angela during her year away, and felt increasingly impatient to see her again.

"Poco is nice, but she's not scientific," Georgina told her mother. "She's in love with a robin. What does that say?"

"That she has imagination?" Mrs. Rusk ventured.

Perhaps Poco felt Georgina's quiet shift away. She looked angry whenever Angela's name was mentioned.

"Of course Juliette is being fed! Anyway, why would Angela care? She wrote me exactly once to ask how her cat was."

"Well, I guess she's been a little busy. She had to learn a whole new language. In Mexico, everyone speaks Spanish, you know. Also, she had to make new friends."

"That," said Poco hotly, "is no excuse. You can't just go off and forget your old ones."

Georgina felt a pang. The truth was, Angela hadn't written to her, either. She hadn't telephoned after the first month. There had been one Happy New Year card. "From Angela," it said. That was all.

"So why *does* Juliette look so thin?" Georgina went on, trying to cover her feelings.

"She doesn't! She looks old. She still goes hunting. Remember last night, how she caught that chipmunk?"

Last night! With these words, Georgina was invaded by a frightening image: seven glass marbles glowing in the dark. She rubbed her eyes to make them go away.

"Well, it's sad to see a cat falling apart. Remember how you used to think Juliette could talk? She must be losing her special powers."

"No she isn't. We still talk if we want. But when people get to know each other, words are less important. They have other ways of saying what they mean. Have you ever seen Juliette with my robin? They are such dear old friends, they've given up words completely."

Georgina shook her head in a helpless way.

"If you don't believe me, come watch. My mother just let Juliette out the back door."

Georgina moved over to the window, where

she witnessed the unremarkable sight of a cat and a bird staring at each other.

Poco sighed. "If you want to know, Juliette is the only reason my robin comes back at all. He likes her ten times more than me. And Juliette adores him, though she's too proud to show it. Neither of them would ever admit it, but anyone can see how they need each other. That, of course, is the true test."

"Of what?"

"Of being friends forever." She didn't have to add, "Unlike Angela." Georgina leapt up and began to get dressed.

Breakfast was under way in the Lambert kitchen when the two girls arrived downstairs. Mr. Lambert was cooking banana pancakes, a Sunday family tradition, while Mrs. Lambert sat at the kitchen table in her bathrobe, giving him advice. Mr. and Mrs. Lambert had clearly not reached the state of friendliness beyond which words are no longer needed, because the whole proceeding was making a lot of noise.

"Well, girls!" Mr. Lambert said, cutting Mrs. Lambert off in midsentence. "A great day for you; I hear the Harralls are home from Mexico."

Georgina's eyes flew open. "Angela is back? But she hasn't called."

"I think it's only since last night. They came in on a late flight from Houston. Not Mr. Harrall, of course. He'll stay on in Mexico with his business. But Mrs. Harrall and Angela are here. And the older brother. What's his name?"

"Martin," Georgina said. "He's going to college."

"I guess that's why they've come tearing home. He has to leave Monday to get to school," Poco's mother said. "You girls are lucky. You have another week." She leaned forward and advised Mr. Lambert to flip his pancakes—unless he planned to serve banana buffalo hide.

"Would you like to take over?" he snapped back.

Meanwhile, Georgina had risen to her feet. "Poco, come on, let's go see her. I can't believe Angela's here after all this time."

Poco didn't answer. She looked at the floor.

"Come on! She'll be desperate to see us."

A scritch of claws sounded against the back screen door.

Poco got up and went to open it. "Will Juliette

have to go back to the Harralls' right away?" she asked her mother in a low voice as the cat passed through.

"I suppose they'll want her."

"Could they at least wait till this afternoon?"

"I'm sure they can. They're probably still asleep. We'll wait for them to call us, okay?"

Poco nodded. She reached out and gathered the big gray Siamese in her arms and carried her to her seat. Mr. Lambert brought over their plates of pancakes. Poco looked dismally at hers. "It's not just Juliette," she murmured.

Georgina had sat back down and was helping herself to a vast sea of maple syrup. The thought of seeing Angela again had suddenly made her very hungry. She could hardly wait to tell Angela about everything that had happened and to laugh and joke around the way they always did.

"There's also my robin." Poco's voice sounded faint. "When Juliette moves to Angela's, he'll want to go, too."

Georgina was in the middle of an enormous bite. "So what?" she asked in a muffled way that came out sounding like "S-wumph?"

After some more chewing, she added, "You

can whawph—I mean, walk—over anytime and seepim—I mean, see him. Besides, he's such a mefferpain, he might not go."

"Such a what?" asked Mrs. Lambert with a concerned look.

"A mefferpain!" Georgina said louder. She paused and swallowed. "Such a featherbrain, I meant. He'll probably forget about Juliette as soon as she leaves."

"Oh no he won't. He'll go with her. The person he'll start to forget is me." Poco raised angry eyes. "I knew this was coming. I've been praying every night that something would happen and Angela wouldn't come home."

"That's awful!" Georgina stopped eating and stared.

"Well, don't tell her, since I guess it didn't work."

"Poor Angela. What will you do now?"

Poco gazed fiercely across the table. "Keep praying, I guess, for something else to happen."

## chapter four

PERHAPS Poco had already prayed enough. Angela showed no interest in getting back in touch. She did not call to ask for Juliette that afternoon, and she did not return the telephone messages Georgina left for her during the next two days.

"Angela hasn't called? Well, that's odd."

The voice on the phone was that of Miss Bone, the Harralls' peculiar old-lady caretaker. She had agreed to stay on, now that the family was home, to act as "cook, chief mop, and bottle-washer," as she told Georgina. "And to look after

Angela, which she doesn't much like. I'm afraid I'm a poor substitute for a mother."

Mrs. Harrall would be back and forth to California. She was trying to transfer to a closer law school, but so far she hadn't found one good enough.

"I know I told Angela you called before, so I suppose she just forgot," Miss Bone said now. "I'm sure she wants to see you. You're her oldest friend."

"Oh," Georgina said. "Well, please tell her again."

But Angela still didn't call back. By Friday, Georgina was frantic. "I'm beginning to wonder if something is wrong."

"Where is she all the time?" Poco wanted to know.

"Out shopping. She needs winter clothes. Miss Bone says in Mexico it's always hot. And yesterday, Angela went to the theater. I stopped by her house, but she was gone."

"The theater! Where?"

"In the city. She went to plays all the time when she lived in Mexico. Angela speaks Spanish just as well as English now."

"How do you know?"

"Miss Bone said so. She said Angela reads books in Spanish, and that she spends a lot of time reading in her room." Georgina's mouth took on a defeated look. In the old days, she had been considered the smart one.

"So she's not always shopping."

"Well, no. But she's busy today because her mother is home. They have hair appointments."

"How horrible."

"And tomorrow they're going to the city for the weekend. Miss Bone says they don't get to spend much time together."

"Oh well. We'll see her when school starts." Poco didn't sound very disappointed. "My mother heard Angela looks completely different."

"Different? How?" Georgina's heart jumped. Angela had seemed so perfect as she was: warm and dependable and loyal to her friends. Though there was one odd thing Georgina remembered. She remembered Angela's face turning angry and red, and how she'd realize suddenly that Angela's feelings were hurt. But when she'd try to make up and ask what was wrong, Angela would turn her back and refuse to answer.

"How different?" Georgina asked Poco again.

"My mother heard she got really tall. And thin."

"Thin!" Georgina couldn't imagine it. The Angela she knew was short and squarish. She was a person who liked to have seconds on dessert, and thirds if she could get them while no one was looking. And she was chatty and bouncy and full of fun.

"And quiet," Poco added. "Someone said she doesn't talk."

On the Saturday before school was to start, Poco saw a picture in the newspaper. It wasn't a very clear picture, nothing that you would stop specially to look at, or that made very much sense even if you did—until you read the words underneath.

New Sightings Reported at
Wickham Reservoir

Members of the Skywatchers, a local UFO watch group, say they snapped this photograph of unknown objects flying over Wickham Dam last week. The group, which was formed to investigate UFO activity in the area, is seeking reports of other alien sightings. "These are not helicopters! Call us if you see anything like them," Skywatchers president Madeleine Toska said. "Something weird is going on around here. We should find out what before it's too late."

Georgina went pale when Poco showed her. She read the story again and examined the photo with pinprick eyes. Then she looked up and said, "She's a fake."

"How can you tell?"

"Anyone who says, 'Something weird is going on around here' has got to be a fake."

"Why?"

"Because it's not scientific. It's stupid."

"But we did see something," Poco insisted. "And the dam isn't far from my house. Just through the woods." She drew the photo toward her across the table. They were sitting in Georgina's kitchen. "It didn't look exactly like this blurry thing, though."

"Like this totally faked picture, you mean," Georgina said. "If we had taken a picture of what we saw, at least it would have been clear."

"But what did we see?"

"Probably nothing."

Poco watched Georgina rub her hands over her eyes. "You don't think we should just tell one other person?" she asked.

"No! No one. Who would we tell?"

"We could call this woman. Mrs. Toska."

"Especially not her. She's a total fraud."

"Well then, how about—"

"I know," Georgina said. "Let's tell Angela!"

Angela was not the person Poco had been about to suggest. She was going to say Walter Kew, their other school friend. He'd had experience dealing with visions. But Georgina was delighted by her own idea. She looked at once relieved and excited.

Poco shrugged. "Well, all right, Angela—if you think she'll care. So far, she hasn't cared even to know we're here."

"She's just been busy," Georgina said. "She meant to call us back, but she kept forgetting. Now this . . . this will get her notice. This will make her remember how much she missed us."

## chapter five

SPEAKING OF visions . . .
"What is that?"
"Where?"
"Over there."
"It's a limo."
"Coming here?"
"Looks like it."
"Who's inside?"
"I can't see."
"The windows are dark."
"It's coming—"

"Watch out!"

"It's coming straight at us!"

The appearance of Angela Harrall at school that first Monday morning of classes caused a great commotion. She arrived like a princess in a white limousine, which did not go around to the drop-off place the way cars were supposed to, but turned boldly into the U-shaped "Visitors Only" driveway out front. Several students were nearly run over. The vehicle swept past like a great pale fish and came to a stop in front of the main entrance. A uniformed driver stepped out and went around to the rear door. He pulled it open and stood aside.

For a moment, there was nothing, just a mysterious dark opening. Then two slim tan legs flashed into view, sporting a pair of eye-catching blue shoes. Next came an arm, a shoulder, a length of dark brown hair, and an intriguing indigo-colored knapsack. A hand reached down to twitch a short plaid skirt into place. The arrival's face was hidden behind her hair.

"Thank you," a voice addressed the driver.

"Yes, miss. See you this afternoon." He drove off, leaving a solitary figure on the sidewalk.

By now, everyone for a good hundred yards around had come to a halt and was watching. Georgina and Poco, who had just walked up, stood gazing as curiously as the others. Poco was about to wonder out loud if a movie star had come to live in their town over the summer when Georgina let out a screech and began to run toward the mysterious person.

"Angela. Angela Harrall!"

This revelation caused an even greater stir among the throngs (more students were arriving every minute) and a whir of whispers and low voices started up. Angela was seen to glance around, startled, and then to focus on Georgina's onrushing body.

"Angela! Hello! Hi! It's me."

"Hello," Angela said. She stepped back to avoid a collision.

"No, it's me!" Georgina seemed about to burst. "Me, Georgina. Your old friend."

"I can see you," Angela said. "You don't have to yell."

"But . . ."

"You're stepping on my shoe."

"Oh!" cried Georgina, who'd been trying to

hug her. "I'm so sorry!" She jumped away. Angela edged back, too. She bent over and rubbed her foot.

"Did I hurt you?" Georgina shrieked.

Angela didn't answer directly. Her hair had fallen over her face again. She stood up and combed it back between fingers whose nails were painted a dashing salon red. "I should go to the office to find my correct class."

"Your correct . . ."

"Shall we catch up later when things are straightened out?"

"What?" Georgina was blinking. "What?" But Angela was already gliding off. Her legs flashed out long and splendid. She slung the indigo knapsack over one shoulder.

"Angela, you've gotten so tall!" Georgina's eyes followed her in wonder.

"I guess I have," Angela's voice came floating back, "because everything here looks so much smaller."

It was the last Poco and Georgina saw of her that day. Angela had not been assigned to their room. They were together in dumpy Mrs. Prout's class. Angela had the new, adorable Miss Glade, but she did not appear with the rest of her class at lunch, or for sports on the playground. And when they got out of school, Angela had gone, though reports of her flew in from all directions.

The white limousine had come to pick her up early. It was said she had an appointment in the city.

"More theater?" Poco asked in a sarcastic voice.

Georgina glanced at her angrily.

Angela had spent the lunch hour in the faculty lounge with Señora Cardozo, the head Spanish teacher from the high school. Several people had overheard them rattling away in Spanish.

She couldn't come out for recess because she'd forgotten her sneakers. Instead, she had been invited to join Miss Heath, the school principal, in her office.

"Miss Heath! What for?" Georgina wanted to know.

"To talk about life in Mexico. Miss Heath used to be a friend of her parents." This tidbit came from Walter Kew, who had happened to be in getting a permission slip signed. "Angela gave Miss Heath a present."

"A present!" Georgina nearly choked. "I didn't know they knew each other so well."

"I don't think they did, at least not up till now. Now Miss Heath absolutely loves her. The present was a beautiful handwoven belt. You know, the ones that have all the bright colors?"

Georgina was hurt and disgusted. "She didn't bring any of us anything."

"She doesn't know me," Walter said.

"No, that's right." Nobody had known Walter back in the days before Angela left. He had been one of those quiet, dopey outsiders—until Poco had met him and made him one of them. Poco never minded having outsider friends. Except now she seemed to mind Angela coming back in.

"Angela was never a nice person," she announced in a chilly voice as the three began their walk home from school. "The one time she wrote me from Mexico, she told me that Poco means 'little bit' in Spanish."

"Angela's in my room," Walter confessed. "It's true that she doesn't say much. Rachel Carfell heard she's been asked to be a model."

Georgina looked sick. "A model! By who?"

"Someone from a big modeling company. They send out scouts to find the right type. Angela got found walking along a sidewalk."

"*Where?* Here?"

"In the city, I guess."

Georgina felt a need to rub her eyes again. It all seemed so unbelievable.

Poco sniffed. "There's the real reason Angela doesn't have time for us."

"Well, I don't care. I'm going to see her. I am going right now to knock on her door. If she's not home, I'll sit down and wait."

"Georgina, you can't. It's not polite."

"I don't care. Something's wrong. Angela's not like this. If you ask me, it's not even her."

Walter looked interested. "You mean she's been replaced?"

"Well, I don't know!" Georgina screamed at him. "How should I know? She's just acting wrong." She turned and stamped away down the street.

Walter's pale blue eyes wobbled a bit. No one could upset him so fast as Georgina. Warily, he peered around at Poco, as if she might decide to turn on him, too. But she reached out her hand and pulled him along. "Come on, let's walk. Don't bother with her. Anyway, I've got something important to tell you."

"You do?" Walter gazed at her thankfully.

"Yes. Do you believe in aliens?"

## chapter six

WALTER did believe in aliens. He believed in a lot more than that. Ghosts, spells, invisible powers—he was used to dealing with the unimaginable. He was an orphan who'd been left as a tiny baby in a casserole dish on Mrs. Docker's front porch. With so much of his family open to question, the unknown was like an everyday companion to Walter.

"Flying marbles?" he asked mildly when Poco described them. "How high up would you say? And were they spinning?"

Poco explained. She told him about the Sky-watchers at Wickham Dam and Mrs. Toska as they walked along the sidewalk toward their homes. This was the same sidewalk that Poco and Georgina had walked home on with Angela before she'd gone to Mexico. The Harralls' big, elegant house was not five minutes past Poco's plain middle-sized one with the broken garage door. Georgina's family, the Rusks, owned a ranch-style house two blocks over.

Walter lived in a tiny house with the paint peeling off, just around the corner from Poco. By now, Granny Docker had become so old that she no longer noticed when things needed fixing. Not that she was in any danger of "passing on to her next world," as Poco said so often of Juliette. But she did not bother with appearances anymore and concentrated instead on the insides of living. Usually, Walter went home directly after school to have afternoon milk and cookies with her. "Granny says she can't be sure what kind of day it's been until she's heard my side of the equation," he explained.

Today, when Walter came to the place where he and Poco ordinarily parted company, he didn't part. He just kept walking.

"Now I think about them all the time," Poco was saying about the flying marbles. "I see them, for some reason, floating in my mind. Want to come in?" she added. They had arrived at her front yard.

Walter nodded. He was pleased to be invited, and not only because of the strange marbles. He kept his eyes down and did not look at Poco as they walked around to the back steps. Walter was fond of her but did not like to show it.

"My idea," Poco said as they went into the kitchen, "was to call Mrs. Toska. Angela is not the right person to tell. She's not interested in investigating things anymore."

"It looks that way," Walter agreed.

"The best thing for Georgina to do is leave her alone. Snooty, rich people like Angela can be very hurtful."

Walter nodded again. He hoped he didn't look foolish, agreeing with everything Poco said. Was Angela snooty? He wasn't sure.

"Mrs. Toska can tell us what the Skywatchers do. Georgina thinks they're frauds, but . . . what do you think?"

Walter attempted a farseeing squint. "Maybe they are. But then again . . . maybe they're not."

This came out sounding so utterly spineless, even to his own ear, that his face burst out in a hot pink blush. He backed away into the living room to hide it.

"Good idea!" Poco shouted to him. "You pick up the phone in there and listen while I call Mrs. Toska. I've got her number right here in the newspaper."

The amazing thing about Poco was that she never seemed to notice that anything was wrong—not blushes or squints or wimpish agreements. She treated Walter with an easy friendliness, as if he were just like everyone else.

Walter sat on the couch and picked up the phone. Mrs. Toska herself answered. At first, she wasn't very nice.

"Is this a child?" she asked in a rude voice.

"A child?" Poco said. "Why do you say that?"

"Well, it sounds like someone trying to imitate a child."

"Well, it isn't," Poco told her definitely.

Mrs. Toska became more pleasant after that, and she explained how she had to watch out for insults. There were people who thought her silly and childish. The Skywatchers were a serious research group that met every Friday at 9:00 P.M. on Wickham Dam, weather permitting.

"Permitting what?" Walter asked later, after Poco had hung up. "I'm still not clear about what goes on."

"Permitting them to see flying objects, I guess. I decided not to bring up the marbles we saw. Mrs. Toska is sort of the nervous type."

"But why on a dam?"

"It's Wickham Dam. You know the stories. There's something about the reservoir that draws things to it. Lately, people have been reporting a lot of sightings."

"Sightings?"

"Well, no one really knows what they are. I think we should go. What do you think?"

Walter felt the weight of Poco's gaze fall on him.

"We could walk through the woods this Friday," she said, moving closer. "I know the way. My parents take me over sometimes in the summer."

Walter began to jump up and down on one foot. This was the kind of behavior that tended to break out when he hung around Poco for too long. As usual, she didn't notice.

"We should set up a plan," she was saying, with studiously bent eyebrows. "I'll call George and see if she wants to help. It would get her mind off Angela."

Walter began to hop on the other foot. "Why does Georgina care so much about Angela?" he asked. He flapped his arms out in a winglike way. It seemed right somehow, and helped him keep his balance.

"They used to be friends," Poco replied. "Before we met you. Now Georgina can't give her up."

"It's sad how people never seem to like each other in equal amounts," Walter panted. "There always seems to be one person flapping—I mean, trailing along after the other."

"That's true." Poco looked toward the window.

"And the other person hardly even knows they're there. . . ." Walter watched as she examined the apple tree. "But the person keeps trailing along anyway, hoping maybe something will change."

"Yes," Poco murmured. "Do you think it ever does?"

"I don't know!" Walter said. By now, he was breathless. He wished he could stop his ridiculous jumps, but they rose up as uncontrollably as hiccups. Not that it mattered. Poco's head was turned away. She'd thought the whole time they were talking about her robin.

## chapter seven

UNTIL SHE met up with Angela outside the school that first morning, Georgina had considered herself a tall person.

"A regular beanpole," people had always called her, and it was true that her skirts were invariably a little too short. Her wrists hung out the sleeves of her sweaters. She was put in the back row for school photographs, and forced to file on stage first for choral performances. Most of the boys in her classes were shorter. Just last spring she had surpassed petite Mme Mianette, the lower school French teacher.

"And she wears high heels," Georgina said with pride.

Poco, of course, had long ago been left in the dust.

"What size are your feet?" Georgina had asked her one day, glancing with a superior eye at the two tiny boots standing under the yellow rain slicker hanging in Poco's locker.

"Ten," Poco said.

"Ten! But they couldn't be. That's bigger than mine." Then Georgina understood. "Oh, you mean baby sizes!"

"I guess so." Poco didn't care about such things.

Georgina's feet were six and a half, adult size, and she had considered that quite exceptional. Ahead of the pack is how she thought of her feet, in the lead, like Georgina herself.

On the way over to Angela's house, Georgina looked down at her feet and for the first time found them wanting. She couldn't help wondering how big Angela's feet were. Size eight? Or maybe even nine. They would need to be that big to go with Angela's legs, those long, tan, ribbon-thin legs that had stepped so elegantly out of the limousine.

Georgina was about to stop and give her own legs a new appraisal (she had a feeling they were too thick, especially around the knees) when Angela's house reared into view. It seemed to have a hundred windows and appeared much larger and fancier than she remembered. The grass was freshly cut along the wide stone walk leading to the front door, and new flower beds had been dug on either side. No plants had been put in yet, but the dirt had a rich, expectant look.

Georgina rang the big lighted doorbell. There was a long wait. Normally, she would have rung again, and knocked. Georgina didn't like to stand around. But something this time pinned her hand to her side. Her eyes rose up to the broad, gleaming windows of the second floor, where—what was that? She saw a shade move. But at that very moment, the door opened.

"Yes?" It was Miss Bone, with her hair tied up in a cloth. She sneezed, then held up a giant feather duster. "Georgina! Good heavens. You've caught me amidst a storm. I was just taking a whack at the dining room curtains." Tendrils of dust drifted off her clothes.

"Hello, Miss Bone. Is Angela here? I know you said she was busy, but . . ."

"I'm so sorry. I believe she's left."

"Could I come in and wait?"

"She won't be back until dinner, I'm afraid. She and her mother . . . but you already know. She does want to see you. Perhaps when her mother's gone. You girls must get together soon."

Georgina heard a light tread on the stairs inside.

Dislodging more dust, Miss Bone turned to look. "Heavens, my dear! I had no idea you were home."

The door was flung wide. Angela loomed in the opening.

"Hello, Georgina." It was hardly a welcome.

"Angela! I'm sorry if this is a bad time, but I just had to see if . . . if . . ." Georgina faltered.

"Please come in." Angela stepped politely aside.

Miss Bone smiled. "Well, here you are, then; no sooner said than done. I'll excuse myself and go back to my curtains. I imagine you two have some catching up to do. If you hear falling bodies, don't bother yourselves. It will just be me in the throes of suffocation."

Georgina laughed as Miss Bone marched off, brandishing the duster like a battle sword.

Angela did not look amused. "Do you mind if we stay here?" she asked, pointing toward a bench in the big front hall. "The house is being painted. We have workmen everywhere."

"What about your mom? Weren't you going to the city?"

"She had to leave early, so I couldn't go."

They sat side by side, stiff as logs. Georgina smelled the reek of turpentine and fresh paint. From some distant reach of the house came a murmur of voices and radio music.

"Is your room being painted?"

"Papered," Angela said. She pulled her long hair back with a practiced hand.

Georgina stared. This new, tall person must be Angela Harrall. And yet even up close, she looked drastically changed. Her face had lengthened and sleeked down around the cheeks. It was so different that Georgina found she no longer knew how to read it. Was this Angela angry? Was she sad?

"Don't you like it?" Georgina asked about the wallpaper.

"Why wouldn't I like it? I picked it out."

"You just don't seem very excited."

"Wallpaper isn't something you get excited about."

"Angela . . ." Georgina paused. She was about to say that the old Angela always got excited about things like new wallpaper. She wanted to ask Angela what was wrong, why she was acting so strange, why they couldn't run around her house the way they used to instead of sitting here talking like two wooden puppets.

Georgina glanced down. The blue shoes Angela had worn to school were gone. In their place was a pair of long-tongued clogs, with a black web of straps that wound up her legs. Georgina had never seen anything like them, and a little wave of fright broke suddenly inside her.

"Have you heard about the alien sightings at the reservoir?" she asked.

"No." Angela stared straight ahead.

"People say they come at night and hang over the water. Some dogs have disappeared, and a doll flew out the window. Poco and I thought we saw them one time. Alien spaceships, I mean. They looked like marbles."

Angela turned. "What did you do?"

"Well, nothing," Georgina admitted. "Later, we thought they were probably something else. There's a group called the Skywatchers that's been formed to keep watch. They meet at the dam on Friday nights—in case the aliens try to come down."

Angela gazed at her. She looked tired. The skin around her eyes was puffy and pink. Georgina wondered if she'd been crying. In the background, the painters' music rose to a wail, placing a new wall of silence between them.

"How was Mexico?" Georgina finally asked.

"Okay."

"Was it hot?"

"Yes. You can't stay in the sun."

"Because you get burned?"

"You can pass out. Once, I couldn't breathe, and I passed out in our yard. When I came to, I was lying on the ground, staring up at a clothesline full of blowing laundry."

"Did you have to go to the hospital?"

"Oh, no. I didn't tell. No one was home."

Angela looked away. "It's just something that happened."

"But you learned to speak Spanish."

Angela paused. "I could when I wanted."

"I bet you felt sort of like an alien yourself."

"What's that supposed to mean?" Angela glared at her.

"Nothing! I only thought you might have."

Angela stood up. "It was so nice of you to come by."

"But Angela!" Georgina was now truly alarmed. The voice that had spoken was flat and false. It sounded like a recorded message.

"And I hope you'll come again at a better time."

"Wait!" Georgina rose, and found herself being ushered toward the door. "Don't you want to help us investigate? The way we used to, remember, before you left? We made a promise to watch out for invisibles, and things that can't be explained, like these sightings."

"Invisibles?" Angela asked with wary interest. "Is that what you're doing now?"

"Yes!" Georgina leaped toward her.

"I remember. We had a name for ourselves. We were going to be investigators of . . . of something." She looked down helplessly from her new height.

"Of the unknown," Georgina said.

"The unknown!" Angela's hand flew to her mouth. "I wonder," she added in a lower tone, "if I still have those strange gold dust letters."

"Get them out. We should take another look."

"You know what? My father still says he never put in the gold dust."

"He does? Oh, Angela, now you sound like you again!"

And for a moment, there did seem to be a glimmer of the old Angela. From somewhere incredibly far off, a spark of her old spirit flew in and hovered just out of reach. Her thin face showed a bit of color and her eyes flashed with excitement and curiosity. But then—*zip!*—in the next instant, her manner changed back to being cool and distant.

"The trouble is, there's so much going on right now, with our moving back here and fixing up the house. I really don't have time to play."

"To play!" Georgina was stung.

"And Mother is leaving next week for California."

"Mother!" Georgina gazed at her aghast. The

Angela she knew had never called her mom that. None of them would think of using that word. *Mother* was the term older people used for the mothers they no longer needed, the mothers that had been outgrown or lived apart in another town. "But isn't your mom—I mean, your mother . . . isn't she ever coming back?"

"Well of course she's coming back! She's only going for a month."

"A month! But Angela, that's terrible!"

A weary look passed over Angela's face, as if Georgina were a small, bothersome gnat that had somehow gotten into the house and refused to fly off, even with the door open. And the door was very much open now.

"Good-bye, Georgina." Angela posed with her hand on the knob, waiting for Georgina to pass through. She looked lofty and beautiful, exactly like a model.

"How tall are you now?" Georgina asked.

"I don't know," Angela said. "Does it really matter?"

She didn't wait for Georgina to answer. With a whir and a click, the door swung closed. Georgina was left staring at an enormous brass knocker.

And now a thing happened that was worse by far. For the old Georgina would never have allowed this sort of treatment. She would have reached out and taken hold of the brass knocker and knocked her way back into Angela's life. She would have shouted at Angela, told her to wake up and to stop using that horrid recorded voice.

But even before the door closed, a new Georgina was stepping into the old one's place. Now, without a word of protest, this new Georgina turned and crept away down the stone walk. She slunk off home with a burning face and her dry eyes itching. (What was wrong with them, anyway?) And no worm in the Harralls' new flower beds could have felt so small and low as she felt walking along, or so weak and discarded, or so helplessly changed by the terrible changes in Angela.

## chapter eight

"THE THING about aliens is, they fly in quietly and take people over before they realize what's happening," Poco was saying to Walter. "I found a book on them at the library. It says they might even be walking among us. No one can tell for sure."

A school week had passed. It was Friday afternoon. They were on the sidewalk, trudging home again. There is nothing like a sidewalk for private conversation. Walter spoke beneath the roar of passing traffic:

"So you think these marble things have landed?"

"Probably not. No. Not around here. They couldn't land here without somebody seeing. Deserts and mountaintops are the usual places."

"And reservoirs?" Walter asked, with an uneasy look.

"Well, not ours," Poco assured him. "Mrs. Toska's got it covered."

It had become impossible to talk of anything else. All week, they had imagined the transparent spheres. That night, there was a chance they might really see them. They were going to meet the Skywatchers at the Wickham Dam. Mrs. Lambert had been persuaded to let Walter spend the night. He would sleep in the guest room. Georgina would sleep in Poco's room, as usual— if she came, that is. There was some question.

"I think these aliens want to land," Poco went on. "They want to come down and understand our world. That's why they float up there and watch, to be ready to land if the right time comes."

"But they're nervous," Walter said. "They don't want to get caught. What if they came down and then couldn't get back?" He adjusted the knapsack he was carrying on his shoulders.

"Well, I guess they'd die, because they couldn't live here. This place would be much too different. They probably couldn't eat the food, and they wouldn't understand half of what was going on. They couldn't speak the language, either, which means if anyone spoke to them, they'd most likely end up being discovered—even if they had taken over a human body."

"That's true," Walter said. "Someone would know. I've seen it on TV—they never act normal. Their eyes have this way of rolling back in their heads, or they hiss like snakes when they get mad."

Poco shivered. "Aliens scare me."

Walter shifted his knapsack again. Inside were his toothbrush and pajamas and a change of clothes. The thought of spending an entire night at Poco's house made him feel a little like an alien himself. Would he have to ask if he wanted to use the bathroom?

"Is Georgina coming?"

Poco shrugged. Georgina was not her usual self. She had hardly spoken to Poco all week.

"She said she might not. She's been feeling sick."

This information made Walter feel both better and worse at the same time—better because Georgina usually upset him, but worse because if she didn't come, he would be alone with Poco. He felt the twitch of a jump come into one leg.

But, after all, the afternoon went by smoothly. Poco was building a "birdominium" for her robin. It was her term for a bird condominium. Birds needed larger homes when they spent the winter. The usual birdhouse was a miserable one-room hut built by someone who had never been a bird and had no sense of bird comfort, she explained.

They rummaged in the garage. There was a hammer and nails, and a stack of ancient twig-colored shingles. Poco set to work on a floor and walls. Walter looked on with a helpful expression.

"How do you know this robin will be living here at all? Don't robins always fly south by nature?"

Poco said, "My bird would never leave without Juliette. They've made a pact to be together forever. And now that Juliette is staying with us . . ."

She stopped hammering and looked up. "That's the great thing—did you hear? Juliette isn't going back to the Harralls'. My mom finally talked to Angela's mother."

"What happened. Didn't they want her?"

"Not until later, if Mrs. Harrall moves back. Right now, she's always coming and going and no one ever knows what her schedule will be. Miss Bone wanted Juliette, but Angela said no. She said an old cat would be too much trouble."

"That's strange. I'd think she would really have missed her."

"The other Angela would have, before Mexico. Now she doesn't have time for pets."

"But why? What happened down there?"

"Angela turned into a selfish person. I heard that nobody liked her at school—which you can see why if she acted like this. And she hated the food and wouldn't eat, so she kept getting thinner, and then she got sick. By then, she'd been so mean to everyone that no one even cared a bit. But whenever her mother called to ask how she was, Angela would lie and say everything was perfect."

"But where was her father? I thought he was there."

"He was, but his job is important, you know. He couldn't be watching her every moment."

"Poor Angela. How do you know all this?"

"Georgina found out. She talks to Miss Bone. And Angela isn't poor. Her family is rich. Why do you think she rides around in that limo?"

At this moment, their conversation was interrupted. Poco's robin flew in with a feathery flap and the subject matter veered toward condo construction.

"Should we put in a bathroom?" Poco asked the bird. "Or would you rather keep taking your showers outside?"

In the end, Georgina decided to come. She arrived at the Lamberts' house with her sleeping bag and a halfhearted look on her face at about 6:00 P.M., just in time for dinner.

"Well!" said Mrs. Lambert, trying to cheer things up. "We're certainly going to have a party!"

At this juncture, Poco asked her mother if after dinner they could walk to Walter's house to watch a movie.

"You mean alone?"

"Yes."

Everyone nodded. This was their plan for getting to the dam, a place they would never otherwise have been allowed to go at night. Poco guessed her mother would not want to bother Walter's grandmother, who was rather deaf (even with her new hearing aid), by checking up on the phone. And Walter's house was only around the corner.

Mrs. Lambert, however, looked wary and surprised. "I'm not sure about this. What time will you be home?"

"We promise to be here by ten-fifteen at the latest," Poco said. "We only have to walk one minute to our door. If we get scared, we'll call you, okay?"

This remark threw Mrs. Lambert completely off the track. She immediately began to worry that they would try to be brave when they were really terrified. She remembered how frightened she had been of walking outside in the dark as a child, and urged them to call her at the tiniest twinge of fear. "I'll come get you! It wouldn't be any trouble!"

In the meantime, she forgot to inquire any more into exactly what movie they would watch, or whether Walter's grandmother knew they were coming. Indeed, she felt absolutely content that she was the best and most watchful mother on earth. Georgina was shocked to see how easily she was fooled. Mrs. Lambert had always seemed so clear-sighted.

## chapter nine

AND NOW, with the expedition to Wickham Dam about to begin, all thoughts of other problems were pushed to one side. The small group had no sooner stepped outside into the night when the vast black vault of the sky opened over their heads, drawing toward it all their concentration. For the first time in weeks, Poco forgot her robin.

"Look!" she cried, pointing. "A crescent moon." It looked like a silver horseshoe flung over the horizon by invisible hands.

Walter forgot his shyness and awkwardness

around Poco, and walked out into the dark like any normal person—that is, looking nervously over one shoulder.

Even Georgina managed to escape from the heavy shadow of Angela for a while and regain a bit of her old confidence. She took up her usual position in the lead, and the three set off in single file through the woods, escorted by a flashlight and flickers of moonlight. They had not gone far when they came upon a well-worn neighborhood path that turned in the direction of the reservoir.

They saw the glint of water through the trees from a long way off. Soon, the sloping bulk of the dam loomed into view. Poco, who knew the way here better, stepped in front and took them around a point of shore to where a narrow stone staircase led sharply upward. Wickham Dam was not very large and had nothing modern or technological about it. In fact, in daylight, one of the dam's main charms was how old and vine-ridden and abandoned it was. And how silent. Especially now! From somewhere, the investigators heard a faint trickle of water; otherwise, the place seemed eerily removed from the normal town noises they were used to hearing.

They had no sooner reached the top of the stone steps and walked out on the dam, however, than they saw headlights across the way and heard a series of car doors closing. An old parking lot was there, barely hidden by trees on the other side of the dam. Another flight of stone steps led down to it, and from this the tramp of feet suddenly rang out.

"The Skywatchers," Walter whispered, and so it was. Silent bands of shadowy shapes began to climb toward them, accompanied by the bobbing yellow eyes of flashlights.

The friends stopped where they were, and jumped up on one of the dam's thick walls, where they sat, nervously, feet dangling down. As they waited, they looked out across the reservoir, and were struck by its powerful dark beauty—the almost-invisible water, the mysterious line of shore, the black body of the surrounding forest. Above, low on the star-speckled horizon, glowed the crescent moon that had accompanied them through the forest.

"No wonder they like to come here," Walter said, and Poco and Georgina knew whom he was talking about.

Then, very quickly, people were all around

them, and over the rustle of feet rose the soft rumble of voices trying to be quiet. Then came the sharp *sh-sh-sh* of someone attempting to keep control. The friends knew that sound from school corridors. They turned around to see the teacherish profile of a fluffy-haired woman carrying binoculars. It must, they supposed, be Madeleine Toska. As they watched, she spoke.

"Please! We must have silence!"

Gradually, the rumbling died away. All eyes turned toward the reservoir. Many in the crowd had been there before and knew without coaching where to look. For newcomers, Mrs. Toska made a short speech explaining the sorts of things to watch for—lights in a pattern, quickly turning or pulsing "stars," a sudden stillness or weight to the air. Poco shot a glance at Georgina. It sounded so like their experience in the apple tree.

Stationed as they were in the very center of the Skywatchers, the three children began to fill with excitement. Even Georgina was affected, though she did not approve. There was the clear sense that things were on the move . . . would be there soon . . . were arriving . . . now!

But then nothing happened. Time elapsed.

The moon drifted an inch lower. From below came the lap of invisible water.

In the midst of this breathless pool of silence, a loud explosion suddenly went off. Poco jerked so hard she might have fallen if Georgina's hand hadn't leaped out and grabbed her.

"Georgina! What *was* that?"

"Someone coughed."

"What?"

"A cough, that's all." Georgina was smirking.

After this false alarm, the sky lost some of its high mystery. Minutes passed with terrible slowness. Around them, the Skywatchers started their shuffling and muffled talking again. And though Madeleine Toska hissed for quiet, it was soon clear that the spell had been broken.

People began to slip away. From the parking lot came the sounds of car doors slamming, of motors grinding into action. The night that had seemed so full of promise would open no window on the unknown this time.

Georgina was heard to snort. "Come on," she whispered. "Let's get out of here." Poco and Walter followed her, downcast.

"The luck of the draw," Mrs. Toska was telling people as the three passed her on the way to their own side of the dam. "Come again next Friday. Patience and watchfulness are rewarded."

"But what if the aliens fly in on a Wednesday or Thursday?" a woman asked her, rather reasonably under the circumstances.

Mrs. Toska's eyes snapped with impatience. "Of course, you may come whenever you like. We Skywatchers work together, so our sightings are official."

Just then, Poco caught sight of a face.

A flashlight beam had played up over the crowd, shining on the tops of heads and sparking off eyeglasses. Suddenly, it stopped and rested in place. In that instant, Poco saw the pale model's brow of Angela Harrall.

## chapter ten

ANGELA.

There could be no doubt. Poco saw Angela's dark hair falling smoothly to her shoulders. She saw the ruler-straight line of one of her cheeks. She saw the sophisticated tilt of her head, and her wary eyes caught out by the light. They were turned exactly in Poco's direction. Then, Poco knew that Angela had seen her, was looking straight at her, cool and attentive. She'd been watching them all for some time, Poco thought, spying out from the tower of her new height.

"Georgina, look!"

The face was gone. A mob of bodies eclipsed the spot where it had been. The light beam was hurled in another direction. And Poco was so short.

"Poco! What's wrong?" Walter saw her jumping up.

"I thought I saw something."

"Well, what?" Georgina looked at her angrily. "Stop leaping like that. You're knocking into everyone."

"I think I saw Angela. Over there."

"Angela!" Georgina spun around. The crowd was still thick and chaotic, and though Georgina was taller than Poco and Walter, she was not yet the height of most of the adults. She could see no farther than a few feet. After some desperate leaps of her own, she pushed her way back to the dam's high wall. Clambering up, she stood on the top.

"Can you see her?" Poco stood wide-eyed below.

"No."

Walter said, "Call her name."

Georgina yelled, "Angela!" But there was no answer. She climbed down, embarrassed.

"Wait," she ordered. "Let's just wait."

They huddled to one side of the dam while the

Skywatchers' ranks thinned slowly into the parking lot. Five minutes went by, then another five. There was no sign of Angela or anyone like her.

Poco consulted her watch under the flashlight. It was after 10:15. They were already late. But Georgina still would not give up.

"She must have come through the woods like us," she was saying. "It's the only way from our side of town."

"Not if you were driven," Walter pointed out.

Into all their minds came the vision of Angela's limousine, rippling through the dark like a piece of white satin.

"Come on," Georgina cried. "Let's check the parking lot."

They ran across the dam and peered down, but most of the cars had already driven away. None of those left was white or long.

Poco said, "We have to go."

"Oh, all right!" Georgina started back toward the stone steps. "All this fuss for nothing. I'm sure you made a mistake."

"It looked like Angela's face."

"But why would Angela have come here?"

"I don't know."

"So, how did she look?" Walter asked.

"All lit up. She was watching us."

"But why?" Georgina could not bear it. Ignored by Angela for two solid weeks, and now, in the dark, to be spied upon? It was maddening! More than that—it was strange. Georgina's heart gave a skip of alarm.

Poco felt nervous, too. "Come on, we have to go!" She grabbed Georgina's arm.

"Okay, okay. I'm sure it was nothing."

"Nothing," Poco agreed. "It wasn't even her."

"Of course not," Walter said. "How could it have been?"

Outright panic seemed now to descend, and they turned and ran headlong down the steps to the woods.


There was no more time that night to think about the eerie specter of Angela Harrall at Wickham Dam. On the back porch of Poco's house, a far more menacing figure rose to meet the friends as they broke clear of the forest and entered the yard. It was, unfortunately, Mrs. Lambert.

"You deceitful things! Where have you been?" She strode in a fury across the lawn. "I called Mrs. Docker. She said you'd never come."

It was a ticklish position to be in. At first, the

friends were tempted to concoct another story to cover up the one they had already concocted. But in the end, their powers of invention failed and there was nothing for it but to tell the truth.

"The Skywatchers! That foolish group?" Mrs. Lambert could hardly believe it. "I would have thought you children had more common sense."

By now, they had all begun to think the same thing. Poco squirmed and glared at Georgina. It was she, after all, who had made them so late. Walter tried to slide off into the shadows. Somehow, these actions angered Mrs. Lambert even more. As a result, the sleepover at Poco's house was canceled.

Poco was ordered into her room. Georgina and Walter were rudely driven home. Mrs. Lambert returned and stamped upstairs to bed, where Poco heard her name brought up harshly to her father. To be talked of in such tones when she wasn't even there—Poco's eyes filled with tears.

Silence came at last to the house. Then—a faint mew from the backyard. *Juliette*—left outside in all the confusion. Poco crept downstairs to let her in.

The poor old cat was sodden with water. She came dripping into the kitchen and immediately set about licking herself off. Poco tried to help with a dish towel.

"Juliette, you deceitful thing! Where on earth have you been!"

Poco's heart was softer than her mother's, though. One soggy cat glance and Juliette was forgiven. "It's all right. What happened? Did you fall in?"

It did look exactly as if Juliette had been swimming, which was odd, because usually she never went near water. Like most cats, she had a special dislike of it. And where would she have found enough water to swim in? No one in that neighborhood had a pool.

Sitting on the kitchen floor, Poco suddenly narrowed her eyes. There was only one place the old puss could have been.

"Were you at the reservoir?" she whispered. But Juliette, being a cat, did not have to tell the truth about anything she'd done. With a secretive shrug, she rose to her feet and sauntered upstairs to lay claim to her bed.

## chapter eleven

WHATEVER the friends had been hoping to see in the black air above the reservoir, it could not compare to the mystery that now began to swirl around Angela Harrall. As the next several weeks of school wore on, they followed her movements with watchful eyes. No one dared to ask her about the dam, or to make any other friendly approach. Poco's sighting weighed on their minds.

Had Angela been taunting them? Was she somehow connected to the Skywatchers? Why had she hidden when she knew she'd been seen? Or maybe it hadn't been Angela at all.

"What if," Walter said, "it used to be her but now she is an alien walking among us? Remember the night she came home from Mexico was the same night you saw those floating marbles."

"Good grief! That's ridiculous," Georgina sputtered.

Poco said, "Walter and I have been reading a book. It says that aliens can take people over."

"That is the most stupid thing I've ever heard."

"Why?" Walter asked. "She's done it to you."

Georgina opened her mouth to protest, but then she looked embarrassed and closed it.

They were sitting on the jungle gym at school, waiting for the lunchtime recess to be over. Around them rose the babble and shriek of the playground.

"There she is." Walter pointed across the cement. They all looked. Above the throngs, Angela stood tall and motionless, a mystery ship moored in its own harbor.

Poco said, "You know, I'm sure it was her. At the dam, I mean. I'm positive."

Georgina looked away. "I guess she was meeting her friends the aliens. Except they forgot to come and take her home, and now she has to go on walking among us."

She was joking. In a way, they all were. Even Walter did not truly believe what he'd said. And yet, the more they watched Angela that fall, the more like an alien she seemed to become.

She dressed in a style unfamiliar to their school: long skirts, hoop earrings, bright fashion blouses—when every other girl her age wore sweaters and jeans. With a self-conscious lilt, she strode along the halls, her head a head above all others.

"I can't believe she's still only eleven!" Poco's mother exclaimed after catching sight of her one day. "She must have a new interest in boys."

"No, she doesn't," Poco said. "She doesn't care about them. She's pretending to be a model, but no one believes her."

"How very odd," Mrs. Lambert said.

It was odder than that. Far more unsettling than Angela's appearance, to her old friends at least, was her manner. There was no other way to describe what she did than to say that she walked and talked like an adult. It was as if she had decided to stop being a child, had shed that skin and stepped out of their world.

She never ran in the halls the way they did, never jumped or screeched, never got excited. In class, while everyone wiggled and fidgeted, or waved their arms to be called on, she sat at her desk with her hands folded.

"Angela? Can we hear your views?" Miss Glade would ask from time to time. (Walter reported on such things.) And Angela would glance up and clear her throat, then speak like one grown-up speaking to another. From somewhere, she had acquired a certain tone of voice, low-pitched, controlled, respectful. Miss Glade was so impressed by this pose that she never stopped to wonder if anything was wrong.

"A lovely child!" she was heard to exclaim. "So well brought up! So polite."

Too polite to be real—every other child knew that. In the minds of nearly everyone at school, Angela Harrall was a faker and a show-off.

Feuds, jokes, in-group remarks—two years ago, Angela had been part of them. Now, as in the beginner's Spanish class she was forced to sit through (a scheduling mistake the school would fix soon), she looked on from a distance, silent and haughty. Left to herself—and she often was—she studiously read a paperback novel or arranged her possessions importantly around her. The word went out that she wanted to be a lawyer.

"Like her mother?" Poco asked.

Walter said, "Well, she acts as if she's already going to law school. I watch when she comes in our room in the morning. The first thing is, she never says hello. She waits till you say it and looks surprised. Then she goes to her desk, takes her things out, and puts them in their special places."

"Their special places!" Poco said. "What do you mean?"

"Her notebooks are always stacked on the left; her tissue box is on the right; her three lucky stones with the white rings around them are all in a line across the top of her desk."

Poco made a face and said, "Scary."

"Then she takes out this battery-powered pencil sharpener and sharpens absolutely all her pencils. She has twenty-five because they came in a pack. After that, she picks five to use that day and lays them down on top of the notebooks. Then she checks her shoes in case they've gotten smudged—and if they have, she wipes them off with a tissue. Then she fixes her hair—she's always doing that. And then she sits and stares at the clock."

The friends looked aghast at Walter.

"She sounds like a robot," Poco said.

Georgina bit her lip but didn't comment.

"Is she really a model?" Poco wanted to know.

Walter shrugged. "Who can tell? She never talks to us. She only hangs around with teachers and grown-ups."

"The snob," Poco said.

Georgina finally spoke. "I asked Miss Bone why she does that. She said it's because Angela wants to be loved."

"Loved!"

"It seems to me she wants the opposite."

"I know"—Georgina shrugged—"but Miss Bone thinks there might be reasons behind it. Like being a child in Angela's family doesn't get you noticed, so Angela's decided not to be one anymore."

"How stupid," Poco said. "You can't stop being what you are."

Georgina sighed. "Miss Bone said that's why it's so sad."

Sometimes Poco and Walter did feel sorry for Angela. It must be hard to be this lone ship of a person, day after day, without a friend to confide in—especially when you had been somebody else.

"Somebody who was fun and popular," Poco said.

Walter mused, "I wonder if she ever remembers how she was?"

"Oh, she does." Georgina suddenly sat up. "She told me she remembers her gold dust letters. And she said how much she wished—" But here Georgina's voice broke off.

"Wished what?" Poco and Walter asked together.

"Nothing," Georgina said. She rubbed her eyes. "I'm allergic to something—that's what my mom says."

"It's Angela," Poco said angrily, and at such times she could not feel sorry for her no matter what the reasons were. "Forget about her, George. Just give up."

But Georgina wouldn't. She kept trailing along behind, hoping against hope that Angela would change. One smile and she would have rushed to her side. One tiny word. One telephone call.

Georgina would have listened and helped her make friends, and tried to explain her peculiar habits. ("Of course Angela worries about her shoes! They were a present from her mother on her last birthday. See, she doesn't get to be with her mom very much.")

She would have protected Angela from the rude remarks that more and more often rang out in the halls.

"Here comes the royal princess."

"Look! It's a giraffe."

"No it's not. It's a lamppost, stupid."

"So Angela, tell us, can you still speak English?"

If Angela was hurt, she never showed it. She never gave anyone a second glance. She stared straight ahead as she walked down the hall, and didn't answer when Georgina called out to her.

"Don't be sad, George. It's not only you." Poco couldn't bear to see her hurt. "It's the way Angela is now. It's not your fault."

"I know." Georgina tried not to mind. She knew with her head but not with her heart.

Impossible as it seemed, things began to get worse. Georgina felt the space between her and Angela widen. It became like outer space, so huge and cold that Georgina was afraid she'd never get across. She trailed farther and farther behind. Angela became a distant moon, and then a faintly gleaming star. There were days when Georgina no longer looked for her, or if she looked, she stopped herself from caring anymore. Even a heart can travel only so far.

And then, strangest and most disturbing of all, one dark November night, Angela really did vanish.

## chapter twelve

MISS BONE was the last person to see her. She served her supper at 6:00 P.M., chicken and rice, and Angela seemed to like it. Her mother had been scheduled to call. But she hadn't, and Miss Bone told Angela not to mind. She'd probably been busy writing a paper for law school, or perhaps she had to go see one of her professors.

It was hard to tell if Angela did mind or not. She went upstairs to her room after supper. At some point, Miss Bone heard the television go on. No one else in the family was home. Angela didn't come out to say good-night, which sometimes she did do, though often she wouldn't. She was known for being an independent girl, not someone to bother other people for attention.

"I'd been told," Miss Bone said later, with a tissue to her nose, "I'd been specially told I mustn't interfere too much."

She looked in on Angela about nine o'clock. The light was out. The room was dark. It seemed she'd put herself to bed. She'd been used to doing that in Mexico.

The next morning, Angela was late for breakfast. Miss Bone went upstairs to fetch her. It was nearly eight o'clock when she knocked on her door.

"Angela! You'll be late for school. Come on. Spit spot. Fifteen minutes till the limo comes!"

There was no answer. Then Miss Bone opened the door and saw with a gasp the bed that hadn't been slept in.

At Georgina's house, the telephone rang at 8:15, while the Rusk family was rushing to eat breakfast.

"No," Georgina heard her mother say into the phone. "How strange. No, she's not here. Just a moment, I'll ask."

Mrs. Rusk placed her hand over the receiver.

"Georgina, do you know where Angela could be? It's Miss Bone at the Harralls', and she sounds upset."

"Isn't she there?"

"No one can find her."

Georgina's eyes lighted up. "Maybe she decided to walk to school."

All the way to school, Georgina kept a lookout. She expected to see Angela walking up ahead, or waiting for her on their old corner. But she wasn't anywhere along the sidewalk, and at school, when the bell for class rang, Angela's desk in Miss Glade's room was empty.

"I don't know where she is," Georgina had to say in a pitiful voice to Miss Heath, the principal. "Before she left, we always walked together. Ever since she came back . . . Oh it's all my fault!" Georgina blinked fast and hid her face.

"Your fault! Oh, no." Miss Heath patted her hand. "I'm sure there's a reasonable explanation. Angela is such a reliable girl."

"It's because I stopped caring. She had no one left."

"She's the one who stopped caring," Poco reminded her later.

At school, no one said a word about what was

84 •

going on. Most people didn't even know Angela was missing. Maybe they thought she'd just stayed home. A teacher frowned at Georgina when she saw her whispering to Poco and Walter in the hall.

"I don't think they want us telling," Walter said.

Poco nodded. "Until we know what really happened. It wouldn't be good to start spreading rumors."

"What rumors?" Georgina cried. "It's a fact. Angela's disappeared from her house."

"Anyway," Poco said in a soothing way, "I'm sure she's all right. She certainly knows how to take care of herself."

"Why does everyone keep saying that!" Georgina wailed.

After school, they walked fast to Angela's house and found that usually quiet yard in turmoil. Three police cars were parked in the driveway, and a crowd of people milled around on the grass. Everyone looked tight-faced and frightened. An investigation of the bushes around the house was under way. Miss Bone was walking about and pointing things out to a man in a raincoat.

"Her window was open," the friends overheard her say. "But I can't imagine Angela climbing down. Too high, and look at that nasty ledge. If she'd jumped, she would have hit it." The man stopped to write this down on a pad.

"But," Miss Bone added when he was done, "I can't see how she went out the front door, either. My bedroom faces the stairs to the hall and, being a light sleeper, I would have heard her."

Word came in from Mrs. Harrall. She was on her way, changing planes in Chicago. She'd be there no later than eight o'clock that night. They'd already had a message from Mexico. Mr. Harrall would arrive as soon as he could. Even Martin was being escorted home from college. For if Angela had been kidnapped (and there was some talk), might he not also be in danger?

Kidnapped! Poco glanced at Walter. She had not thought of Angela being dragged away. She had thought of her deciding to take the day off, or of going, high-and-mighty, to some modeling job and forgetting to leave Miss Bone a note.

"Georgina? Did you hear? They think Angela might have been kidnapped."

Georgina's face was an odd color.

Walter said, "If she was, it was probably to

get money out of her father. That's why the police are here. I bet they've tapped the phone and now they're waiting for the kidnappers to call."

Just then, a phone did ring somewhere. It seemed to come from one of the police cars. The crowd on the lawn stopped milling and froze. Three police officers leaped toward a man wearing earphones. He sat in his car, with the door swung open. Miss Bone came bustling over. She was handed the phone on the fourth ring.

"Hello?"

There was a long and breathless pause.

"Oh yes," Miss Bone said. "No. No . . . no, I'm not interested in center-cut pork."

She gave the phone back to the man in the car.

"Frozen meat," she said, and walked off.

Georgina asked if they could sit down.

"Where?" Poco looked around.

"Let's go outside the yard," Walter suggested. "Somewhere we can talk but still see everything."

They set up an encampment of sorts on a grassy bank across the street. Poco went home to check on her robin. This made Georgina furious. Imagine thinking of a bird at a time like this!

He was fine, Poco said when she returned, though somewhat confused about his new house. He kept sitting on the roof instead of going inside.

Poco had brought back sodas and pretzels. They sat munching numbly and looking at the yard. There was a great deal of coming and going. Martin arrived. Family friends kept dropping by. Miss Bone had to answer every phone call. And each time there was a terrible silence while everyone stopped breathing and nearly choked to death. Not once was it the kidnappers demanding a ransom.

"Why haven't they called if they really have her? By now, almost anything could have happened," Poco said in a restless voice. For Georgina, this was the last straw.

"Shut up," she yelled. "Will you just shut up? I don't think you care about Angela one bit!"

"Of course I do. She was my friend, too!"

"Was!" Georgina shouted. "Are you hoping she's dead?"

The afternoon dragged on. Darkness began to come early—4:30, according to Walter's watch. By this time, it had grown much colder. Their jackets were no longer keeping them warm. Breath misted out of their mouths.

"Well . . . ," Walter said.

"Well . . . should we go?" Poco looked cautiously at Georgina. She didn't want to set her off again.

"Go if you want to. I'm staying here."

"But George . . ."

"It's all right." She wasn't angry. "Could you call my mother and tell her where I am? Tell her I'll be home for dinner at six-thirty."

"Well, okay, if you're sure."

Walter and Poco packed up the empty soda cans and went off.

Georgina sat on by herself and watched. Presently, she moved closer to the front fence. But even that seemed too far away. She wanted to be near in case the kidnapper called. If she could have, she would have worn the earphones. She wanted to hear the kidnapper's voice: "We have her. She is all right. If you'll just hand over a million dollars . . ."

She resettled on the lawn near the Harralls' garage, with her back to a tangle of forsythia bushes. The air began to grow colder. The sky was dimming to a dark metal gray and several lights had appeared in the Harrall house when a low hiss sounded into her ear.

"Psst! Georgina!"

"What?" She whirled around. Angela was crouched in the bushes behind her.

"Angela!"

Angela laid a finger on her mouth. "Sh-sh. Don't tell. I just need to know. Is my mother here yet?"

"No. But she's coming."

"When?"

"About eight o'clock, I think. She called and said she was on the way. Oh, Angela! Are you all right?"

"Yes. I'm fine. I've been . . . somewhere. But they brought me back. I just came from the reservoir."

"Who took you?" Georgina gazed at her. Angela was wearing a new dark winter coat and a dark woolen hat and mittens. Except for her face, she was almost invisible—a shadow hidden within the shadow of a bush.

"Who were they?" Georgina asked. She glanced back over her shoulder. No one on the lawn was watching them. Behind her, Angela rustled some leaves.

"I think they were aliens," she whispered.

"Aliens!" Georgina faced her in disbelief.

"Sh-sh! Listen, I'm not coming out. Not till my mother comes home at least. I don't want to talk to all these people. Especially not . . . Is that the police?" Georgina saw that she was trembling.

"Angela, do you want me to wait with you?"

Angela's glance flicked over her. For a moment, Georgina felt herself being pushed away. Then Angela's shoulders sagged and she nodded.

Georgina could have reached out and hugged her. But she didn't; she kept herself in control. "You look tired. I bet you were up all night. We need to go somewhere safer," she said.

Angela raised her eyes gratefully. "How about the garage?" They were crouching quite close to it. "We could go to Miss Bone's old apartment. It's been empty since she moved into my house."

At this moment, the telephone in the police car rang, and Georgina jumped in fright. But the next second, she began to laugh.

"Angela, we've been so scared. Everyone

thought you got kidnapped and that somewhere someone was keeping you prisoner."

"But that is what happened," Angela said seriously. "Come on and I'll tell you." She began to sneak off.

Georgina followed, swift and silent. The girls crept unseen around the back of the garage and up the stairs to Miss Bone's apartment.

Soon after, night filtered down like a fine black soot, obscuring all remaining detail. In the Harralls' big house, more lights went on upstairs and down. The crowd of people on the lawn drifted home for dinner. The police drove off, leaving behind one man in a car. It was the car with the telephone, which continued to ring out through the dark yard at intervals. But whether Miss Bone answered or someone else had taken over the task, Georgina never knew, because by then the sound seemed a long way off and she was deep in the folds of Angela's fascinating story.

# chapter thirteen

"THEY CAME and got me," Angela said. "They took me away and I couldn't stop them."

Georgina was quiet for a moment. Out in the yard, she heard the telephone begin again. It stopped short in the middle of a ring. "Where were you?" she asked.

They were sitting in the dark. Through the window came a glow from the house across the way, just enough illumination to be able to see dimly.

"In my room." Through the gloom, Angela's

face looked old and pale, less than ever like the child's face Georgina had known before.

"It was after dinner," Angela said. "They turned the TV on."

"How did they do that?" Georgina asked.

"They sent down a beam of light from the sky. That's how they got me. The window was open."

"So then they came in and . . ."

"Took me." Angela sat quite still. "The noise of the TV covered it up."

"Did you scream?"

"I tried to. They were so fast, though. At first, I didn't see what was going on."

"Did it hurt?"

"Yes. I didn't want to leave."

"So then . . ."

"Wait a minute." Angela got up and went across the room to look out the window. Some sort of bustle had erupted out there. A car door slammed, and there were footsteps.

Angela said, "It's my father. He just came."

"Don't you want to go down?" Georgina asked.

"No." Angela turned around and came back. They faced each other on Miss Bone's living room couch, slouched in opposite corners, with their legs folded up. "I can't go down till my mother gets here. She's the one I need to tell. Do you think she'll come?"

"She said she would."

"Well, she always says that." Angela raised her chin. "Then something happens that's more important."

Georgina nodded. "So what next? I guess you were kidnapped."

"I was," Angela said, and her lip quivered. "They swirled me up in a beam of light and flashed me to a spaceship out in the sky. Then we flew to another universe. I looked out and saw our Earth getting small, and I got really scared, but no one noticed. The aliens were too busy flying away. They didn't plan to be mean; they had other things to think of."

"Did you see them?" Georgina asked. "What were they like?"

"They were pale and wispy, like laundry on a line. No bodies like us. Just pieces of cloth. And their faces were wavy and wouldn't stay still, so you never knew when they were looking at you."

"Angela! Is this true?"

Angela stared at her. "Yes, it is," she replied with unmoving eyes.

In that instant, for reasons she couldn't

explain, Georgina felt the metal-hard edge of the truth. It made her think of what Poco had said about friends who invent silent ways of speaking. Angela had just told her something with her eyes that was more than the story coming out of her mouth.

"Go on," Georgina said breathlessly. "What did the aliens do with you next?"

Angela sat back and wrapped her arms around her knees. "I was put in a capsule in the middle of the room, where the aliens could watch me but I couldn't see them. They were off in the shadows, drifting around, but I was in a place where the light poured down and it got so hot, I could hardly breathe, but when I asked for cold air, they couldn't hear because . . . well, it was queer: they didn't have ears."

"No ears!"

"And they talked a different way."

"Like what? You mean like another language?"

"Oh no. I could have learned that. I learned to speak Spanish in just a few weeks. What the aliens talked was completely silent. They didn't have words; they had currents, like wind, that flew back and forth invisibly between them. See, they heard by feel instead of by noise, and that's why their faces and bodies flapped. They were talking all around me, but I never heard a sound."

Georgina leaned back. "So what did you do? How did you talk to them?"

"I didn't," Angela said. She looked down at her hands. "I would try sometimes, but they never understood."

Georgina gazed at her. "Angela! How terrible."

"I know," she said. "It really was. It's so nice," she added softly, "to be telling someone."

After a pause, the rest of Angela's story began to stream out. Her words were so clear and her eyes begged so hard to be believed that Georgina knew with great certainty that she had lived through these things. She described a hundred details of the aliens' spacecraft, which was huge and round and seemed completely made of glass.

She said the sky passing by outside was always dark, as if they were traveling through an endless night. But the spacecraft was kept lit, and she was let out from her capsule sometimes to float around its glistening insides. She had to float because there was no gravity to hold her down.

But much as she tried to copy what the aliens did and how they moved, she would lose her balance and start grabbing on to things. Then they would swoop down in a great rush of cloth and pry her loose and stuff her back in her capsule.

Everyone, including her, felt better when she was in there, so that was where she spent most of her time—time that went at a dreadful crawl. For though by Earth time only a night and a day had passed since she had left, inside the aliens' spacecraft hours expanded until they grew into what seemed like a whole year.

"A year?" Georgina said, looking at her thoughtfully.

Soon Angela started to shiver again, and she told how careless the aliens had been. They did not seem to know how to treat a human child, and took to shrinking her down or blowing her up. Or they stretched her into a long ribbony thing as part of their experiments to see what she was made of.

"Because bodies were not important to them," Angela explained, her face showing the flush of a hidden anger. The aliens were always disappearing into thin air, then returning whenever and however they pleased. This was maddening for someone used to Earth rules, and to people being real and there and touchable.

"The only thing they really worried about was whether or not I was eating," Angela said. "But their kind of food wouldn't go down my throat, so they pumped a lot of strange stuff into my capsule. Whatever I ate, I'd just get sick. In the end, I gave up. It wasn't worth it."

"Were you ever afraid you'd never get home?"

"Yes," Angela whispered. "Yes, I was. I thought the aliens would get tired of me and throw me out one of their spaceship's windows. Then I'd die this horrible death and float around forever like a doll in space."

Like a doll! Georgina was shocked. "Oh, Angela! Don't! You're all right. I think we should go down and tell your father."

But Angela wouldn't. She would not budge. Not that she didn't love her father. "I still do, a lot. And Martin, too." She just had to talk to her mother first.

"Do you think she'll come?" she asked again. "Being kidnapped by aliens is important, I think."

"Good grief!" Georgina said. "Of course she

will. And when she hears what happened and what you've been through, your mom will see how lucky she is you came back!"

At this, for the first time, Angela smiled. "You know what, George?" she said. "I think you almost understand."

# chapter fourteen

LATER,
Angela would tell
her story to others. She would tell it to her
mother first, and then to her father. And after
that to the police, Martin, and Miss Bone—and
somehow, perhaps because the story was so
strong and real, the news of her abduction would
leak out and make its way through the town.

LOCAL GIRL ENCOUNTERS ALIENS? Headlines
with question marks would appear in the papers.
A television station would interview Mrs. Toska
on the subject of Earth safety. Neighbors would
meet and disagree in the supermarket aisles over

"what really happened to the Harrall girl." A rumor would circulate that Mrs. Harrall believed her child and was taking firm steps against the aliens coming back.

Later, Angela's story would spread into the air beyond the town, beyond the state and even the region, and become one of the strange homeless stories that float around the world. Like the little girl's doll that flew out the window, or the disappearing dogs, it would take on a life of its own, acquiring meanings far beyond the original ones.

Later . . . but not now. Now, for a moment more in Miss Bone's old apartment, Angela's aliens were a private thing told between two friends in a place that was apart from other people's thoughts and meanings—even a mother's.

For all the time Angela had been telling her story, she had been gazing more and more warmly at Georgina. Perhaps she saw how closely Georgina listened to every word, and how she never hurried her and always wanted to know more. Or maybe it was the luxury of being able to sit back and talk in your own language to someone your own age who knows exactly what you mean and believes you are important.

Whatever it was, Angela's eyes began to lose their pleading expression and her face relaxed. Her long body began to take on the roll of Miss Bone's old couch. Her voice rose and matched the rhythms of Georgina's voice, and her hands stopped reaching up to comb through her hair.

By the time her story came to an end, she seemed so much like her former self that Georgina felt the rough braid of their old friendship start to weave together again. This, in turn, gave Georgina confidence, and even emboldened her to go a step further. For much as Angela had said she almost understood, there was one last thing Georgina had to clear up. After Angela had rested for a while, with her head leaned tiredly back against the sofa cushions, Georgina asked in her softest voice, "Angela? About these aliens . . ."

Angela cocked her head. "I've told you everything already."

"I know. I just have to find out. Who were they really? You can tell me. I won't say anything, ever, to anyone. Because I see how, actually, it really did happen."

Angela blinked. "You do?"

"I mean, in a way, you were kidnapped to a

hot, alien world all by yourself. And nobody noticed how sad you were, and your parents didn't hear when you tried to tell them because they were so busy with their own problems, and they kept floating off and disappearing and trying to make you eat—exactly like those . . ."

Angela had risen to her feet as Georgina was speaking. At first, she looked startled and seemed to want to interrupt. But then her head turned and her attention went toward the windows, where a noise of car tires could be heard from below. Angela leaped forward and went to look.

"It's my mother!" she whispered. Then she screamed, "It's my mom!" She turned around and stared with wide eyes at Georgina.

"Well, go," Georgina said. "Don't just stand there."

"I can't believe it!" Angela said. "I can't believe she came. All the way from California, and she wasn't even late."

Georgina stood up. "I told you she would."

Angela clasped her hands together. "Oh, Georgina, thank you! For staying and listening and seeing everything!"

"Except you didn't finish saying—" Georgina

began, but Angela was suddenly flying across the room and running full steam through Miss Bone's abandoned kitchen.

"I'll call you tomorrow morning," she shouted back. "Oh, yes, and tell Poco I saw Juliette. She was at the reservoir, hanging out near the dam."

"Juliette? Are you sure?" Georgina asked. It seemed too far for a creature that old. But Angela was already out the door and pounding down Miss Bone's apartment stairs.

Not only was Mrs. Harrall not late; she was a whole two hours early getting home—a miracle that Angela never forgot, but that was also lucky for Georgina. Otherwise, she never would have been back in time for dinner at her own house. Then her mother would have yelled, unless she'd made something up—which Georgina probably would have done if it had come to that, since her mother would have thought less than nothing of the truth. ("Angela asked you to stay? That's your excuse?")

As it was, Georgina still had a little time before she had to start home, enough to spy out through Miss Bone's window and watch as Angela hurled herself into her mother's arms. Mrs. Harrall began crying and wiping her eyes while she held on to Angela with all her might.

Then Mr. Harrall ran out with his tie flapping, and flung his arms around them both. Shortly after, Miss Bone appeared in a long black shawl, which she swept from her shoulders and wrapped like a great winged bat around them all. Only Martin stood discreetly aside—though not very far off—which was to be expected of someone going to college.

Finally, with much sniffling and talking, the whole family went indoors, and Georgina sneaked down and walked home fast.

## chapter fifteen

ANGELA
did call Georgina
early the next morning, just as she had promised
she would. She called to say, in a low whispery
voice, that she wasn't going to school that day
and would call again that night, when the police
were gone.

"Does your mother believe you?" Georgina
asked straight out.

"I think she does, because she's crying all the
time," Angela whispered, but then someone
must have come into the room, because suddenly she said, "Good-bye!" and hung up.

"Sounds like the same old rude Angela to me," Poco said when she heard about it at school. By then, she knew all about Angela's alien story because Georgina had told her on the phone the night before. For some reason, it didn't impress her very much. "At least she called you back," she went on now. "Maybe soon Angela will even talk to me and Walter."

"Yes, she will," Georgina said. "She's changing, I think. She's just got to fix up some things with her mother. That was the main problem before she got abducted."

"Abducted!" Poco sniffed. "I'm not so sure. Everyone I've talked to thinks she's lying."

"Well, she isn't," Georgina said, rising up to defend her. "Angela's telling the absolute truth. If you'd been there, you'd know it, too."

"Maybe I wouldn't," Poco declared. "You certainly are back to your bossy ways."

"Walter believes me. Don't you, Walter?"

He was standing off a bit to one side, shifting his weight and sending Poco worried looks. He had his own opinion but was afraid to say it. At last, he dared to speak up, anyway.

"Well, you have to admit, Angela's alien space-ship sounds exactly like one of those marbles you saw. Round and glassy and all lit up. How could she have known—unless someone told her?"

Poco looked at him admiringly. "Walter, that is so right! I certainly didn't tell her. Did you, George?"

Georgina glanced away. "I don't remember."

"You're trying to protect her, aren't you?" Poco said.

"I am not. Why should I?"

"Because you can't help it. You're determined to believe in her no matter what. And you used to say you were so scientific."

"This has nothing to do with that!"

Walter, meanwhile, had turned a wretched pink after seeing how Poco had appreciated him. And who knows what he might have started doing next, jumping or humming or standing on his head, but luckily the discussion was just then cut short by the nerve-racking clang of the end-of-recess bell.

Before anything more could be determined about Angela's story, another mystery arose. Juliette, the old Siamese, was missing. There had been no sign of her since the night Angela was supposedly beamed out her window. Fearing the worst, Mrs. Lambert had said nothing to Poco, who was too distracted by everything else to notice her absence. But today, when Poco came trudging home from school, Mrs. Lambert felt it her duty as a mother to speak.

"What do you mean?" Poco demanded, standing flat-footed in the kitchen entry. "Juliette never spends the night out anymore. She's too old for that. She always comes back."

"Well, last night, she didn't. And she hasn't all day. You know she hasn't been very well lately. Animals do have a way of going off at the end, and Juliette has always been so independent. I'm afraid this time we must prepare—"

"No, we mustn't!" Poco said shrilly. She fled back outside before she heard any more. Her robin was in his tree, she saw with relief, though he looked a bit down in the wing and beak. And he wouldn't meet her eye when she went by to chat. This was not a good sign, and Poco's heart sank further.

It was only that night on the phone that Georgina, hearing about Juliette, remembered to tell

Poco the message Angela had given her in Miss Bone's apartment.

"At the reservoir!" Poco said, in the same tone one might use if one's blood had frozen.

"That's what Angela said. I'm sorry I forgot to tell you. It didn't seem that important after everything else. Anyway, Angela just called me up again. She wants us to meet her at the reservoir tomorrow. I think she wants to show us where the aliens beamed her down. You can ask her more about Juliette then."

"But I want to ask her now!" Poco shrieked. "Hang up so I can call her right this minute."

"Well, you can't. She's not home. She went out with her mom," Georgina said in such a smug voice—as if she owned Angela, or had more right to her than other people—that Poco herself hung up with a crash.

Only late, late that night, sitting sleepless on the edge of her bed and straining her eyes through the window for the telltale slink and slide of a cat, Poco was sorry she'd lost her temper. She could have used the happy thought of a friend right then. Outside, the night seemed so cold and careless, and the sky whirled overhead so darkly and unknowably, that a sudden understanding rose in her of what pure loss and loneliness were made of. For a moment, she had a vision of Angela spinning through space, cut off from everyone she loved on Earth. Whether that story was true or not, there was something about it that made her shiver.

"Oh, Juliette," Poco whispered, "where are you?"

## chapter sixteen

ANGELA
had said she would
be waiting on the top of Wickham Dam at ten
o'clock the next morning, which was a Saturday.
And there she was, her slim shape standing high
up in the distance. Walter saw her first and
pointed her out to the others.

The three had met at Poco's house and walked
through the wintry woods, this time with Mrs.
Lambert's permission.

"Do I trust you?" she'd asked, putting an eye
on each child in turn. "You won't fall in the water
or go too far and get lost?"

"Of course not!" Poco said. "We're not stupid."

"Well, with four of you there, I suppose you'll be all right. I'm so happy to hear you're meeting Angela."

They had all been eager to meet her, even Poco a little. But now the sight of Angela's tall figure looming above them—they were just approaching the dam's stone steps—sent an uneasy feeling through everyone, recalling the eerie night that Poco had seen her there. They climbed the steps more breathlessly than usual.

Angela heard them coming and was waiting at the top when they arrived.

"Hello!" She looked flushed with excitement. "Hi! Hello!"

For a moment, they all felt shy and embarrassed—to be together so abruptly after all the time gone by. But soon, the strangeness began to wear off. For one thing, Walter Kew had to be introduced.

"I remember you!" Angela exclaimed. "You once brought a Ouija board to our second-grade room."

"Oh yes," Walter said. "You thought I was a creep."

"No I didn't! I was scared. The whole class

was. We thought you were a witch or a sorcerer or something."

"Well, now he's one of us," Poco said, tight-lipped.

"Listen," Angela went on, "before anything else, I want you all to know you're invited for lunch. It's my dad's idea. He's going to make tacos."

"Your father! Is he still here?" Poco looked most suspicious.

"He's staying over in Miss Bone's apartment. Until he has to leave, that is, sometime next week. But he's coming back to live near us. He says he likes our weather here better than Mexico's."

"What about your mother?" Georgina asked. "My mom said she's moving back and quitting California. And she'll go to law school here even though it's not as good."

"That's right," Angela said, glancing down. "She's decided she likes our weather better, too."

Poco said with a sudden rudeness, "What you mean is that you've scared them both to death by running away. And now they'll never dare leave you alone for an instant."

"Poco!" Georgina cried. "Will you shut up?"

But Angela asked quietly, "What's wrong with that?" She meant scaring parents, not Poco's rudeness.

"Nothing, I guess." Poco looked at her. "Except it's a mean and selfish way to get attention."

But Angela looked back with complete serenity. "It wasn't me," she insisted. "It was the aliens who did it."

There was a pause after this while they all caught their breath. Then Angela said, "Come on, I'll show you where I landed."

They set off across the dam, Angela in the lead, and went down the stone steps on the other side. The old parking lot was there behind the bushes, but before they came to it, Angela veered off to the right. She went into a grove of fir trees, up a little hill, and down again.

"I hope we don't get lost," Walter said, noticing how the tree branches closed in back of them.

"We won't," Angela sang out. "I know this place. We'll come back soon to the reservoir."

The trees thinned a few minutes later and, just as she had said, a clearing opened that allowed them to see out across the reservoir. A group of large boulders occupied the clearing's center, looking almost like a small fortress. Angela walked straight over and sat down against one of the rocks.

"Here we are!" she said. "This is it."

Everyone's cheeks were bright with cold by this time. Though the sun was out, the air was freezing.

"You landed here?" Walter asked doubtfully.

Angela nodded. "It was late afternoon. I could see the sun going down over there." She pointed up toward the dam, visible in the distance through a screen of protruding tree limbs. "If you crouch here, you can stay pretty warm."

Poco sat beside her with a skeptical glance. "Did the aliens just throw you out, or what?"

"I came down the same way I went up, I guess. In some kind of light beam that made my head fuzzy. When I finally woke up, I figured out where I was. That's when I saw Juliette," she added.

Poco's head whirled around. "Here? Where was she?"

"Down there by the water."

"I'll go check," Walter said, and ran off.

"She looked as if she was waiting for something," Angela continued. "You know how cats hunch down and pull in their paws? I went to say hello, but she didn't get up."

"Hello!" Poco cried. "You should have brought her home. She was probably sick and couldn't walk. Can you see her anywhere?" she called to Walter.

"She's not here now," he yelled.

"No," Angela said, "she wasn't sick at all. In fact, she was looking sort of younger, and happy. She kept watching the sky and purring to herself. I patted her for a while, but then I had to go."

"You left her alone? That was bad, Angela."

"But Poco, she could have come. She knew who I was. She was waiting for something else. So I said good-bye. It was what she wanted."

"Good-bye?" Poco's eyes glistened with tears. She turned her head away to hide them.

Walter had come back up the slope from the water. "I think I know what she was waiting for," he said.

"What?" Poco peered around.

"For night," Walter said. "To get picked up."

"Picked up! By who?" Suddenly Poco's face changed. A flicker of hope streaked across it.

She glanced over desperately at Angela. "Angela Harrall, is this really the truth? I have got to know absolutely. You saw Juliette waiting here? And she was looking up at the sky and purring?"

"I did," Angela said. "I promise. Cross my heart."

"So it might have been . . ."

"The aliens," Walter whispered. "Look what I found down near the water." He took Poco's hand and put in her palm the little collar Juliette had worn. Hanging from it was the tiny silver box.

"I can't believe it," Poco said. "And there's still dried catnip inside. Whew! I'd know that smell anywhere. I guess the aliens didn't like it either."

"Oh, rubbish!" Georgina muttered under her breath. She'd believe in Angela's aliens but not anyone else's. Angela was looking quite amazed herself, but Poco and Walter didn't notice. They were standing together, gazing happily up.

"The unknown," Poco was saying to him. "It's always there, hiding out where it's never expected. I knew Juliette would leave, but not with aliens. She certainly is going to another world."

"Where I hope they feed her better than they fed Angela." Georgina's sharp eyes rested on her friend.

In the bright sunlight, Angela looked so beautiful. Her long, dark hair was flooding down her back, and her cheeks had turned rosy from the wintry air. She was almost too fine, Georgina thought, and a low, wormish feeling crept into her heart.

"Is it true you're a model?" she asked fearfully. "We heard you got discovered."

Angela laughed. "Good grief, I'm too young for that. I found out you have to be fourteen at least, and starve yourself, and wash your hair all the time. I intend to get fat and sloppy, and have fun. Speaking of which, lunch! I almost forgot. Come on!" Angela jumped up. "My father's going to need a lot of help."

"Oh, Angela," Georgina said, as they walked away, "I'm so happy you came home. It was terrible without you."

"Was it? I'm glad." Angela smiled and took her arm. "I'm planning to stay forever, in case you want to know."